Dear Parent:
Your child's love of reading starts here!

Every child learns to read in a different way and at his or her own speed. Some go back and forth between reading levels and read favorite books again and again. Others read through each level in order. You can help your young reader improve and become more confident by encouraging his or her own interests and abilities. From books your child reads with you to the first books he or she reads alone, there are I Can Read Books for every stage of reading:

SHARED READING
Basic language, word repetition, and whimsical illustrations, ideal for sharing with your emergent reader

BEGINNING READING
Short sentences, familiar words, and simple concepts for children eager to read on their own

READING WITH HELP
Engaging stories, longer sentences, and language play for developing readers

READING ALONE
Complex plots, challenging vocabulary, and high-interest topics for the independent reader

ADVANCED READING
Short paragraphs, chapters, and exciting themes for the perfect bridge to chapter books

I Can Read Books have introduced children to the joy of reading since 1957. Featuring award-winning authors and illustrators and a fabulous cast of beloved characters, I Can Read Books set the standard for beginning readers.

A lifetime of discovery begins with the magical words "I Can Read!"

Visit www.icanread.com for information on enriching your child's reading experience.

I Can Read!

READING 2 WITH HELP

DREAMWORKS

MADAGASCAR

ESCAPE 2 AFRICA™

AIR PENGUIN

Madagascar: Escape 2 Africa: Air Penguin
Madagascar: Escape 2 Africa™ & © 2008 DreamWorks Animation L.L.C.

Library of Congress catalog card number: 2008926056
ISBN 978-0-06-157764-2

Typography by Rick Farley

❖

First Edition

DREAMWORKS

MADAGASCAR 2

ESCAPE 2 AFRICA

AIR PENGUIN

Adapted by Gail Herman

Pencils by Charles Grosvenor

Paintings by Lydia Halverson

HarperCollins*Publishers*

The animals from the New York zoo are leaving Madagascar.

N.Y. or Bust

"You've been a great crowd!"
Alex calls to the lemurs.
"Good-bye! Good-bye!"
say Marty, Melman, and Gloria.

Skipper and the penguins stand
at the controls of an old airplane.

"Doors?" asks Skipper.

"Check!" says Kowalski.

Vacation in Madagascar? Over.

Mason and Phil, the chimps,
don't look up.
They're too busy playing chess.

"This is your captain speaking,"
Skipper tells everyone.
"We'd like you to sit back, relax,
and hope this hunk of junk flies!"
Rico gives the signal.

Lemurs cut the vines.

Boing! The plane flies up

like a slingshot.

Who says penguins can't fly?

Over Africa, Kowalski spots trouble.

A red light flashes. Danger!

"Rico!" Skipper orders.

"Instruction manual!"

Rico hands over the book.

Skipper smashes the light with it.

"Problem solved!" he says.

Boom! One engine goes out.

Boom! The second engine goes out.

Something is wrong,

and it isn't the light!

"Buckle up, boys!" says Skipper.

"We're coming in for a landing!"

The plane crashes through trees.

The wings and the tail rip off.

The airplane drops.

"Ahhhhh!" scream the animals.

Quickly the penguins open parachutes.

Whoosh!

The plane floats to the ground.

"Hey, happy slappers!" says Alex.

"The plane is a wreck.

How are you going to fix it?"

"With grit, spit,

and a lot of tape!" Skipper says.

17

People on a safari tour ride past.

"They'll help us," roars Alex.

But no one understands his roaring.

"You're a bad kitty!"

says a mean old lady named Nana.

18

"Who needs people?" Skipper says.

"We're penguins!

We need airplane parts.

And a plan!"

The penguins get an idea.

"We'll take a truck!" says Skipper.

Private pretends he's been hit.

Screech! The truck stops.

"He's hurt!" says the driver.

The people rush out of the truck.

The penguins jump into the truck.

"Good work, boys!" says Skipper

as they drive away.

The penguins take more trucks.

They strip off metal.

They pull out plugs and wires.

Now they have

plenty of parts

to fix the airplane.

23

But it's not easy fixing a plane
when you have flippers.
"Where are our thumbs?"
says Skipper.

Just then, Phil and Mason show up.

They have thumbs!

Their friends have thumbs, too.

"Well, I'll be a monkey's uncle,"

says Skipper.

Suddenly, Marty gallops over.

"The plane!" he pants.

"Need it! For a rescue mission!

Alex is in trouble!"

But the plane isn't ready.

The penguins need more spit here

and more grit there.

And lots and lots of tape!

Can it be fixed in time?

At last! The plane is ready.

Everyone gets into place.

The penguins put on snappy music.

The chimps eat bananas

to help them power the propellers.

The engine roars.

The plane flies over the trees.

The chimps help Alex escape!

"It's you!" Nana yells

at the penguins.

"What did you expect?" asks Skipper.

"A barrel of monkeys?"

Now everyone is safe.

The penguins fly the four friends

back to the water hole.

Mission? Complete!

"Thank you for flying Air Penguin,"

Skipper says.

"Now sit back, pipe down,

and enjoy the trip!"